THE

PRISONER

**He's About to Learn What
Real Punishment is Like**

A hard BDSM series by

ELI HARDER

Copyright 2017 by Eli Harder

ON A PERSONAL NOTE:

I have always searched for BDSM erotica that is very severe, functionally torture, but not permanently damaging and still has an element of caring and comforting. Usually stories turn out to be too fluffy and soft for me, or if they are harsh enough, they cross the line into mutilation or unrealistic things that could never be done to a human body without serious harm.

It appeared that if I wanted hard-core punishing BDSM that didn't degrade into a borderline snuff film at the hands of a Dom evil enough to have been dragged out of a lair, I was going to have to write it myself. Here you go.

DISCLAIMER:

This is a fictional punishment manual, and while it expresses concern that the titular prisoner not suffer long-term injury, the practices within it HAVE NOT been certified as safe by anyone. Do not go out and try these things on your partner. If you are tempted to, you should at a bare minimum consult with experienced BDSM experts to see if they consider the activity safe and sane for use on actual human beings that exist in the real world.

THIS IS NOT A MANUAL FOR "PUNISHING" YOUR PARTNER!

IT IS EROTIC FICTION ONLY AND NOT TO BE USED IN THE REAL WORLD.

CHAPTER ONE

Decision Time

Newly life sentenced felon Neal Landon's hands were shaking as he sat in a windowless cement solitary confinement cell facing the rest of his life. Confinement, control, boredom, and tedium, for eternity. He was only 27, and the idea was unbearable.

The only reading material he'd been allowed all week were the papers he was currently holding. They detailed entering the infamous Life Sentence Diversion and Rehabilitation Program.

It was actually one of the US Marshals who'd bussed his chained-up and crying ass across the state who'd held up the one glimmer of hope. "Might be able to get into the aggravated dog training program," said the Marshal with a hint of droll humor, sitting down on a spare seat across the aisle from him.

"The what?"

"Life Sentence Diversion and Rehabilitation Program. More like torture program, or aggravated dog training. They strap an electric dog collar on you and train you like one for a few years, stopping now and then to beat the shit out of you an' yank on your balls until they let you go. That's the thing right there, they let you go."

The sinking feeling in Neal's gut deepened, but a tiny flicker of hope surfaced. He'd actually heard of that program through a series of outraged news articles detailing the horrific way inmates in it were treated.

"Oh." Neal didn't even know how to respond to horror and hope battling it out for control of his mind.

"How violent are you?" asked the Marshal. "They don't take rapists, murderers, pedos, wife beaters, anything like that."

"Robbery and kidnapping," said Neal. "Haven't hurt or killed anyone, ever."

Neal had masterminded a kidnapping for ransom where the victim hadn't been ill-treated, let alone raped. He'd stolen 15 ATMs in one night, loading them on a truck and removing cash. He'd robbed two banks. He'd stolen a speedboat and led harbor police and finally the coast guard on a chase just to feel like James Bond.

"Well, you look young and fit," said the Marshal. "You might make it in if you don't got any medical issues."

"Do they really release life sentence inmates?" asked Neal, hope starting to win.

"Yup." The Marshal shifted in his seat and looked thoughtful. "Most of us didn't approve, at first. But they got a recidivism rate of something like, one percent? Lower than any corrections program in history."

<<<><>>>

When Neal arrived at the maximum-security prison he was to die in decades from now, he asked his horrified lawyer, Mark Barrett, to try to get him into the diversion program.

"It's the worst human rights abuse our justice system has ever conceived of!" spluttered Barrett.

"I'm going to die here in thirty to seventy years," said Neal. "This prison has a literal hospice ward. As the human whose rights would be abused, I'm thinking it sounds like a way to be able to drive a car and see the ocean and eat good food again."

<<<><><>>>

It was a month later, and as far as Neal could tell, he was eligible as long as his blood work came back okay. He'd passed the battery of physical, fitness, and psychological tests.

"You opt into the program, you waive your rights against cruel and unusual punishment irrevocably," Barrett had warned him in the visitor's room a day ago, when Neal was given these papers.

"I know," said Neal.

Another man was with them in the dimly-lit, dingy visitor's room. His name was Alan Tansey, and he was an agent of the Life Sentence Diversion and Rehabilitation Program.

"It doesn't allow prisoners to be permanently injured, but it's intense physical and mental punishment," said Tansey in a mild voice.

His lawyer, a strong supporter of human rights, disliked the program and obviously hated the agent. Neal didn't mind the guy so far; he was an intelligent-looking sort with an understanding gaze and a blunt manner of speaking.

Barrett sighed. "Neal.... you were sentenced to life in prison. Five days after you got here, you stole a CO's radio and landed your ass in solitary. Those aren't actions of a guy with one iota of impulse control. How you gonna do in a program where using the toilet without permission will get you beaten?"

Neal cringed internally. "Very, very badly. I'm going on the assumption I'll be pretty much tortured, most of the time. It just sounds better than never having the chance at a life, ever again."

Tansey, the agent for the program, spoke up. "Actually kid — yes, it'll be harder on you than you can possibly imagine. But most prisoners in our program have close to zero impulse control, it's why they're in prison in the first place. The program trains people to control their impulses and behavior. It works."

"You know a lot about this," said Neal. "Would you go through it, if you were facing a life sentence?"

Tansey gave him a nervous smile at the thought. "I can't even imagine having to make that choice, having seen the suffering prisoners go through. But yes, I probably would simply because I would have a life again when it was over. I'm not recommending it to you, Neal. It's hell, and you should only do if if life imprisonment is the most intolerable thing you can imagine."

"How — exactly does it work, getting a handler?" asked Neal.

"When you're accepted into the Life Sentence Diversion and Rehabilitation Program, you're transferred to our training center where you'll be shock collared and taught basic rules and verbal etiquette. This basic work is done by trainee handlers learning how to work with real prisoners," said Tansey.

The agent gave him an intense look, something in his expression saying, I'm trying to help you. "There'll be four or five handlers at any given time who have an opening for a prisoner, and they hang around the training center watching and choosing a prisoner they they'll be able to develop rapport with."

In other words, your future handler will be watching.

"And when I get chosen?" asked Neal. "Are there better handlers and worse ones?"

"Of course," said Tansey. "We have experienced, brand new, and so-so handlers, like any large employer. To attract an experienced handler who's genuinely good at rehabilitation, you're gonna have to show him you're submissive to orders and eager to please."

"So experienced is good?" asked Neal. "Doesn't that mean they'll be better at, uh... punishing me?"

Neal liked the idea of a novice handler, possibly sympathetic and reluctant to hurt him too badly. In prison, new COs were usually far kinder than veterans.

"New guys are bloodthirsty and go after the knuckleheads they want to fight and break," said the agent. "That's usually the best match for both of 'em. Experienced handlers look for a guy who's already trying. Training a prisoner is hard work for years of your handler's life. They want you to be worth it."

"Do I have the same handler the whole time?" asked Neal. That sounded both reassuring and terrifying. One single person controlling his every move for years? But if he'd spent a long time with one person at the center of his universe, it could suck to be thrown at the mercy of a stranger.

"We try for that," said Tansey. "Handlers quit, retire, get sick, and even get fired like everyone else. But handlers and prisoners usually bond, and develop trust and caring over the years. Everyone tries not to break that."

"Do they take vacations?" asked Neal, curious. Retiring and getting fired sounded like such ordinary, job-like things for someone who was essentially a professional torturer.

Tansey chuckled. "Yes. Either another handler takes care of you, or you're kept at the training center. I don't want to make the program sound rosier than it is, but in late stages of rehabilitation handlers have been known to take their prisoners with them on vacation."

"What happens after I get a handler?" asked Neal.

"He takes you home," said the agent. "Most handlers live within a day's driving distance of the training center. Handlers' basements are modified with cells and punishment—"

Neal's lawyer cut in. "Torture equipment. Just fucking call it that, okay? You have something called the rack, and you strap prisoners to it so you can strip them naked and beat them," snapped Barrett. "You've fucking institutionalized basement torture chambers."

Tansey rolled his eyes and continued, unfazed. "Punishment devices. They often let prisoners eat with them, have them do household chores, and let prisoners sleep on a small bed on the floor of their bedroom when those privileges are earned."

"Wait - so how many prisoners does my handler have at a time?" asked Neal.

"One," said the agent. "You're your handler's full-time job. You'll spend a lot of time locked up, but you also get to be in a house and go outdoors which is perhaps the only way the program is more enjoyable than prison. Your handler will punish you, train you, and generally put you through more pain and stress than you can imagine, for your foreseeable future."

"That actually sounds like a really expensive program," said Neal. The Corrections Department was as cheap as they come, so that surprised him.

"It's cheaper than a life sentence," said Tansey bluntly.

"Is it possible to flunk out?" asked Neal.

The agent nodded. "You'll be failed out if your handler doesn't think you can be rehabilitated, if you commit a crime on the ineligible list, or you manage to piss off your handler so much he doesn't want you any more."

"What happens if I fail out?"

"Back to the training center to be a human practice dummy for new agents learning how to punish prisoners. It's much, much worse than the diversion program."

Tansey looked grim, and rubbed his forehead. "Failed prisoners are there for years, because the program has fewer failures than it has handlers to train. When you're too much of a wreck to be useful, you're dumped back here to complete your life sentence."

"Sounds like I don't want to fail out," said Neal with a shudder.

Tansey gave him an actually sympathetic smile. "It's honestly very hard to fail out. We make it that punishing so prisoners don't consider misbehaving to get out of the program when they realize how bad it is."

"Listen to that, Neal," warned his lawyer. "You're essentially signing up to be a serial killer's torture toy in his basement, minus the serial killing."

Tansey folded his hands. "I'm going to leave you with this. You haven't known misery until you've been in severe pain for months, are so physically and emotionally exhausted you can barely stand, and your handler puts you in a bit that gags you, hitches you to a cart, cuffs your hands behind your back, and makes you haul gravel for the city in the snow all day."

"Are you telling me not to do this?" asked Neal. He liked this agent; he was blunt and seemed both unflinching and compassionate.

"I believe you're a good candidate for our program," said Tansey. "But I want you under no illusions about what it entails, or about being able to handle it because you're a tough guy."

Tansey handed Neal a sheaf of papers. "These are the standard rules, disclosures about the rights you waive, and what handlers are and are not allowed to do to you. The second is written for handlers, but it's useful to see just what you can expect. If you opt in to the program, there's no out. You will have no possessions, rights, or free will for your foreseeable future."

Back in his cell, Neal had a sinking feeling in the pit of his stomach as he read the first document.

CHAPTER TWO

The Rules

COMBINED PRISONER RULES AND WAIVER

Life Sentence Diversion and Rehabilitation Program

For the purposes of the program, prisoners are not "inmates," "clients," or "patients." They are prisoners, and are referred to as such. The person managing you is referred to as a handler. He has absolute authority over you, your body, and your future.

Important note: This is merely a short list of rules that apply to all prisoners and handlers. Handlers are free to (and expected to) enforce far more comprehensive rules and restrictions.

WAIVERS

Prisoners irrevocably waive their constitutional and human rights. There is no right to sue or pursue any legal option against any person or entity regarding the diversion program, even in the unlikely event of serious injury or death.

Consent to enter the program is irrevocable. There is no "way out" or appeal of any kind.

Prisoners are not guaranteed release, from the program or prison. This is under the sole authority of the handler.

Typical time spent in the program ranges from 1-7 years. The longest a prisoner has been in the program was 10 years. The program experiences a mere 1% recidivism rate upon release. Fail out rate is approximately 2%; see below for consequences of failing out.

Diversion Program cells are smaller than legal limits for normal prisoners and contain no windows. You may be confined to them for months or years.

Handlers are allowed to inflict any punishment that does not cause lasting or severe physical harm. There is a general scale of punishments from "mild" to "torture" to be used at their discretion. Prisoners have no right of dissent or appeal.

Temporary physical injury is permitted. This typically includes bruising, welts and abrasions not expected to leave serious permanent scars (typical of beating, invisible tattooing, and use of restraints), and muscle strains.

Prisoners can expect to receive abrasions from metal handcuffs and other restraints which may leave permanent scarring, and nerve damage, in almost all cases temporary, from handcuffs and other restraints. Prisoners are advised to avoid pulling or fretting against restraints even if they are in severe pain.

Prisoners can expect to receive minor scars from being beaten. If your misbehavior leads to a serious or torture level beating, scars will almost certainly form and may be permanent.

WHAT HANDLERS MAY NOT DO TO YOU

Cause serious injury or permanent injury. Example: your handler may not hang you from the ceiling with all of your weight suspended on handcuffs. Your handler may however force you into a stress position where extremely painful pressure is placed on handcuffs.

Break bones, insert piercings (with the exception of suture staples which may be used as punishment), burn the prisoner (other than mild chemical or sun burns), deliberately cause sprains, or damage tendons.

Rape, defined as the handler penetrating any orifice with his penis or causing the prisoner to have contact with the handler's penis, is prohibited. The handler is also not permitted to masturbate in front of the prisoner.

However, handlers are tasked with controlling, and thus punishing often hardened criminals without injuring them. As options for inflicting severe pain without injury are limited, handlers are allowed to punish, handle, penetrate, beat, and otherwise inflict pain on the prisoner's genitals.

RULES

All orders must be obeyed without delay or question.

All rules, both these and those set out by the handler, must be obeyed.

You must cooperate and comply utterly and completely with zero resistance to all restraints, punishments, and confinement.

You must obey strict verbal etiquette when allowed to speak to the handler. Your training will cover this.

You are prohibited from masturbating at any time for the duration of the program.

CRIMES COMMITTED WHILE IN THE PROGRAM

If a prisoner breaks the law, for example by committing theft, attempted escape, or assault on the handler, the handler will report the crime to the Corrections Department.

The Department legal team will evaluate the crime and the typical sentencing within the standard justice system and assign a sentence.

The Corrections Department will relay the sentence to the handler, who will translate it to Diversion Program rules and carry it out. In general:

One year in prison translates to one "Torture" level punishment. If you commit a felony in the program, you will be tortured. Ten years in prison translates to ten "Torture" level punishments.

These are carried out sequentially; typically one per day, however, some punishments span several days or weaken the prisoner badly enough that he needs a week to recover before the next punishment.

One year of probation translates to 24 hours of strict confinement. This means around the clock confinement to the Cell with no comfort items, clothing, or entertainment.

The prisoner will be shackled at all times except when caged for 8 hours per day, and will usually be required to sit or lie motionless in an assigned position when not using the toilet. Lights will be on at all times and the prisoner will be fed only punishment drinks.

These are carried out sequentially with no breaks except for a brief punishment shower every two days.

DIFFERENCES BETWEEN BEHAVIORAL AND ROUTINE PUNISHMENT

Behavioral punishment: Punishment delivered as a consequence to the prisoner's behavior. For example, shocking a prisoner because he disobeyed an order is behavioral punishment.

Routine punishment: Punishment delivered as part of the prisoner's sentence. It is not tied to the prisoner's current behavior.

For example, placing the prisoner in a restraint chair for eight hours directly after they awake is routine punishment. A Mild 10-point beating on the rack once or twice a day is routine punishment.

A good handler will always make it plain whether a punishment is routine or behavioral, and if behavioral, will tell the prisoner clearly why they are being punished.

WORKING HOURS CONCEPT

In general, handlers are encouraged to submit prisoners to at least 8 hours of severe discomfort, pain, or exertion a day as routine punishment delivered as part of their sentence.

This may be in addition to behavioral punishment, and may be inflicted for longer than 8 hours, which is a minimum guideline.

There are no upper limits; this is not a restriction but simply a warning that even prisoners who are being perfectly behaved will receive at least 8 hours of routine punishment daily.

MEDICAL AND DENTAL CARE

Prisoners receive attentive, professional medical and dental care while in the program, with complete exams and workups every 3 months due to the strain the program puts on the body.

Handlers will not hesitate to summon a doctor if the prisoner is ill, has an infected wound, or possible injury in need of care. If you need care, you will be treated with compassion, and medical procedures will not be used to hurt you.

As brutal as he when punishing you, you may be surprised how much your handler cares about your basic well-being and how gently he will handle it if you need treatment. Do not hide medical issues from your handler out of fear.

Painful medical procedures and conditions will be treated with appropriate anesthetic and pain relief.

For example, if you develop a tooth abscess and have a tooth removed, local anesthetics will be used during the procedure and you will be given pain medication during recovery.

You will not be given pain relief for injuries and pain inflicted as punishment.

For example, if you sustain a strained shoulder muscle in a stress position, your handler may call a doctor to make sure no more serious injury is present and to get advice on how to treat you while you recover. However, you will not be given pain medication, even over the counter anti-inflammatory medication. If an abrasion on your wrist from handcuffs gets infected, you will receive antibiotics but not pain medicine.

FAILING OUT OF THE PROGRAM

Prisoners are often desperate to escape the punishing conditions of the program and try to figure out ways of doing so. Thus, the one way out of the program, complete failure to learn, cooperate, or submit, has a far harsher consequence than remaining in the program.

Prisoners who fail out will be transferred to the training center. They are considered not able to be rehabilitated, so their mental state is of no consequence. They will be used as training dummies for new handlers learning punishment techniques.

Because new handlers are inexperienced, they are more prone to injuring prisoners; that's why they practice on failed dummies first. There is no behavioral punishment or reward; prisoners are simply used as a tool at that point.

It is far more painful overall than being in the program; torture punishments are practiced regularly, and the prisoner might for example be placed on the rack and beaten by various trainee handlers for an entire day without relief, then be used to demonstrate severe electric collar punishments all day the next.

Because the program's failure rate is so low, and new handlers join the program regularly, live training dummies are quite valuable to the program and will be retained for as long as possible. When they are no longer able to walk or function mentally, they will be transferred out to die in prison.

Prisoners are advised to obey, respect, and cooperate with their handlers at all costs, as failing out is the worst possible option.

CHAPTER THREE

The Manual

ALLOWABLE PUNISHMENTS AND THEIR LIMITATIONS

*Life Sentence Diversion and
Rehabilitation Program
Guidelines for Handlers*

SEVERITY OF PUNISHMENTS

Punishments are generally rated Mild, Moderate, Severe, and TORTURE. Some ratings are given in this manual, although these are only generalizations.

Mild punishments should be inflicted daily as routine punishment, a part of every prisoner's sentence.

Moderate punishments are used to punish minor infractions.

Severe punishments are used to punish more serious behavioral issues and infractions.

Note that punishments designated as TORTURE are only intended for use to punish severe infractions such as breaking criminal laws, not simple disobedience. See sentencing guidelines for such punishments. Handlers are advised to limit torture punishments to once per day in order to allow the prisoner to recover mentally.

TYPES OF PUNISHMENT

CONFINEMENT

There are three locations the prisoner can be confined when not in the company of the handler: the standard Cell (used for general housing), the Chamber (used for stress positions, punishment, and sleep deprivation), and the Tomb, (used for short-term intense punishment).

All cells contain advanced CCTV camera and alarm systems that allow the handler to monitor the prisoner from the comfort of his house, or on a mobile app. For example, if the handler orders the prisoner to lie motionless in the Cell, a motion sensor can be activated to notify the handler if the prisoner moves.

The electric shock collar can also be controlled by the app when out of range of the remote, making it easy for the handler to control the prisoner when out doing errands.

The Cell:

Resembles an ordinary jail cell, but smaller. Measuring 6' long by 5' wide, it has very cramped quarters. It is made of unpainted concrete, and has a metal barred door; there are no windows.

The bed is a steel platform running the 6' length of the cell. It is 2 1/2 feet wide and sits 18" off the floor. The area under the bed is a barred cage, 6' long, 2 1/2' wide, and 18" high. There is a small toilet at the rear of the cell beside the bed.

At the foot of the toilet, a metal eyelet is embedded into the cement securing a very heavy chain 4' long. The chain connects to a wide, heavy shackle.

Handler has discretion over use of the heavy ankle shackle within the cell, which will cause abrasions, sores, and intense pain with prolonged use. Taking the shackle off at night will make long-term use more bearable for the prisoner while retaining the psychological impact of wearing it during the day.

The cage within the cell is used by opening the cell door, removing the shackle if used, and having the prisoner crawl into the cage. Closing the cell door locks the prisoner in the cage.

Being in the cage is boring, and uncomfortable because the prisoner cannot sit up and is forced to lie on concrete. Prisoners over 6' tall will be unable to stretch out fully. Handlers are able to place bars at the end of the cage if they wish to similarly restrict prisoners under 6' tall, or wish to make the space even smaller.

Handler may additionally place prisoner in the cell wearing restraints such as handcuffs and leg irons. If left on around the clock, the hands must be cuffed in front (may be rear-cuffed for up to 8 of every 24 hours) and such restraints may be used for no more than one week (Severe).

Limits: Prisoner may be kept in the cell for the entirety of their correction, provided they are removed for at least one hour a day and allowed to exercise. This is not encouraged, but it is permitted.

If the prisoner is kept in the cell without any one hour relief periods, such confinement is limited to 30 days (Severe) and must be followed by at least a five-day break where they are allowed relief periods.

If the prisoner is shackled, it must be switched to the opposite ankle every 12 hours to prevent deep pressure sores. The shackle may be used for up to 30 days (Severe) at a time, at which point it must be removed until the shackle sores and abrasions are fully healed.

Confinement to the cage within the cell is limited to 8 hours in a 24-hour period if food, water, or elimination are denied. The cage may be used for up to 4 weeks provided that the prisoner is allowed out for 8 hours at night, and is removed from the cage every four hours for food, water, elimination, and light exercise (Severe).

Neglect and Abuse:

Remember, this is a rehabilitation program. Further, all prisoners in this program have opted for it rather than be confined to a prison cell indefinitely. These prisoners generally fear being abandoned to a cell more than they do the pain of physical punishments. Because we have found that it is a very important control measure for handlers to have the authority to threaten confinement for the duration of the program, we have given you that leeway.

However, any handler who chooses to simply confine a prisoner long-term without working with him is likely to have his prisoner pulled and be terminated for abuse and neglect, unless they have a strong justification for such confinement. Handlers are not paid to ignore prisoners, they are paid to train them.

A prisoner who has been confined to a tiny basement cell with no outside contact or mental stimulation for years is not a candidate for successful re-integration into society; he is a candidate for a mental health facility.

Handlers are allowed and encouraged to use the cell liberally; however, they should also take their prisoner out in society and allow them to sleep comfortably in the handler's bedroom when the prisoner's behavior allows it.

The Chamber:

12′ x 12′ square and 9′ high, the chamber has a solid metal door with no windows. The door is 5 feet wide for wheeling in restraint and punishment devices. All surfaces are painted bright white.

When a prisoner is alone in the Chamber, isolation and lack of visual stimulation produces overwhelming boredom, where literally the only thing available for the prisoner to focus on is his own suffering.

The Chamber doubles as a "torture chamber" for inflicting stress positions and other punishments, and as a solitary confinement cell. It has over 100 hooks and rings embedded in every point imaginable in the ceiling, walls, and floors.

The extra space allows for the prisoner to be restrained spread-eagle on the floor, against a wall, or stretched from the ceiling. It also allows restraint chairs and other devices to be wheeled in, and has plenty of room to swing a beating implement.

Its primary use is for the prisoner to be restrained in painful positions and abandoned in isolation to endure them.

There are light switches outside the door for off, on, and extra bright.

When the extra bright lights are turned on, the Chamber is a blinding, uniformly white box that makes it impossible for the prisoner to accurately evaluate the passage of time or imagine anything outside of the Chamber and what they are experiencing it it. The extra bright lights are also used during sleep deprivation punishments.

Turning the lights off can make the prisoner feel utterly abandoned, and fear that the handler will not return to relieve their punishment, and it also makes the Chamber feel much smaller.

The Chamber is equipped with temperature controls that can effortlessly turn the environment within very hot or very cold from outside the Chamber.

As the Chamber was designed as a space for handlers to conveniently punish their prisoners, rather than for routine, prolonged confinement, it contains no bed platform. It does not contain a toilet. Prisoner may be diapered, provided with a container for elimination, or forced to soil himself if left in the Chamber for longer than he can contain elimination, for example during sleep deprivation.

The Tomb:

A box surrounded by 3 feet of solid cement on all sides except the front, 2 1/2 feet wide by 4 feet long and high. Jagged, sharp stones line the walls, floor, ceiling, and foot-thick metal and cement door. There is no lighting, it is light-proof and soundproof. Air exchange is silent through two small tubes, and it is kept chilled.

Prisoners are stripped and placed in the Tomb for up to eight hours in utter darkness and silence. They cannot stand or stretch out; they can lie down on their back or sides with legs curled, or they can sit.

All positions are painful with bare flesh pressed with the prisoner's weight against sharp rocks embedded in cement.

An easy and very harsh punishment. Combines sensory deprivation, fear, cold, pain, restraint, and boredom simply by closing a door.

Prisoners are generally desperate for release after a half hour in the Tomb. More commonly it is used for an interminable hour or two or three, at which it is common to open the box and find the prisoner shivering from cold and crying in pain and fear.

Limited to 8 hours per day, not more than a cumulative total of 14 hours a week. Six hours is considered an immensely severe punishment. TORTURE at 8 hours.

Caution: Because confinement and restraint are so integral to the program, prisoners with claustrophobia are not admitted. The Tomb has the ability to cause claustrophobia, which could get the prisoner failed from the program.

If a prisoner panics in the Tomb, tearing open their hands, face, feet, and other areas trying to escape (causing real injury), it should not be used again and a program psychiatrist should be called immediately. While awaiting the psychiatrist's arrival, the prisoner should be kept unrestrained in a light, soft area.

Enhancing Confinement:

Bright lights: Usually used in the Chamber, during sleep deprivation or stress positions.

Darkness: The Tomb allows no light entry; the Chamber can also be darkened although there is some very minor light leakage.

Isolation: Denying human contact except for meal delivery.

Boredom: Denying the prisoner television, radio, reading material, or anything else that might help time pass.

Discomfort: Denying the prisoner a mattress or bedding.

Nudity: Leaving the prisoner in the cell without clothing induces a sense of vulnerability, and they will also be cold if left without bedding.

Restraint: Use of the shackle in the cell, handcuffs, leg irons, or other restraints.

BEATING

Beating is one of the most effective correction and control methods as it causes bearable but significant pain and can vary widely in severity.

Beatings not rising to severe punishment or torture levels are recommended as general punishment for the prisoner's initial crime. They may be inflicted without the prisoner having offended in any way, but the prisoner should be reassured that they have not offended.

Hands: (limited to light strap, and flogger). Prisoner's hands may be pinioned and struck on the palms or the backs.

Upper back and buttocks: (no limits, approved instruments and locations only). Use caution with caning (as trained) so as to avoid permanent scarring or nerve damage.

Genitals: (limited to genital strap and genital flogger). Use caution as trained so as to avoid permanent damage or loss of sexual function. TORTURE if severe and/or prolonged causing bleeding, bruising, or swelling lasting more than 12 hours.

Feet: (limited to light strap, and flogger). TORTURE if severe, prolonged, or of sufficient intensity to make it painful for the prisoner to stand the next day. Use care not to cause permanent damage, similar to genital beating.

Other areas: (limited according to handler's detailed training). A flogger may be used on most areas except the face, neck, or genitals. A cane should be restricted to the upper back and shoulders, buttocks, backs of the calves, and the front and back of thighs. Straps may be used anywhere other than joints, spine, face, neck, genitals, stomach, lower back, or any other location where they may cause injury.

TORTURE only if severely prolonged and damaging, especially over large portions of the body. See exemption for feet and genitals.

BEATING, PART 1: THE RACK:

The prisoner may be beaten anywhere, at any time. However, most serious 10-point beatings are carried out on the rack. Made of sealed hardwood, it has a pivoting curved plank 10" wide that the prisoner's body rests on. While it is impossible to fall off once restrained, the narrowness of the support makes the prisoner feel unstable.

With the platform in the vertical position, the naked prisoner is walked up facing it. They extend their arms straight forward, parallel to the floor, and the wrists are captured in leather cuffs which are pulled tight towards a steel t-bar mounted to the underside of the plank. This pressure will increase significantly when the rack is pivoted forward, pulling the prisoner off their feet.

There is a lightly padded hole in the board for the prisoner's face. It is somewhat long as the prisoner's body will slide down when the rack is rotated. The prisoner's ankles are affixed in broad leather cuffs, which are anchored to the floor by straps of a length precisely calibrated to the prisoner's body.

Then the rack is rotated forward 45 degrees. This causes the prisoner to be pulled forward and down, nearly off their feet, and brings the support board in contact with the pelvis.

At this point the prisoner's arms are stretched painfully forward and are also angled slightly above the head, as the prisoner's body weight will have pulled him down as the rack was rotated. Because the board is narrower than the body, the forward and up pull of the arms will have stretched the skin and muscles of the back taut which increases the pain of the beating.

The head is strapped down tightly with the face in the hole so that it cannot be lifted or turned.

A round, sliding anchor peg roughly 9" long and 1" round is mounted in a track at the center of the board. The prisoner's genitals are tucked upwards between the bottom of the board and his body, and the anchor peg is slid up between the prisoner's legs and pressed firmly against the perineum and anus. Then the peg is locked in place.

This prevents the prisoner's body from sliding down further when the rack is rotated again, which could damage his arms and shoulders. Instead his weight will be held (painfully) in place by the peg until the rack is in its final position roughly parallel to the floor. The peg is angled downward so that the tail bone is not easily compressed against it.

A series of thick, 1 1/2" leather straps are anchored to the underside of the support board. They are easy to wrap around the prisoner's torso and buckle.

The first strap goes around the mid to lower rib cage. Its function is to prevent movement of the prisoner's back when they are struck on the shoulders, and mark the line below which the handler should not strike with anything heavier than a flogger to avoid damaging the ribs. This strap should not be over-tightened, because it could restrict the prisoner's breathing. The stretched, slightly upward angle of the arms is already placing mild strain on breathing, so be cautious.

Next is a series of 5 straps placed very close to each other that start just above the hips and end just below the rib cage. These should be tightened as much as possible. They serve as the main anchor preventing side to side movement. They also restrain the back when the prisoner arches in pain, hold the buttocks in place firmly for beating, and protect the kidneys from stray blows.

These will restrict breathing somewhat when very tight, as the abdomen (which is compressed by these straps) usually expands when the prisoner inhales. Check the tightness of the chest strap, and observe the prisoner's breathing.

Next, the rack is rotated forward until the prisoner's legs come in contact with the lower portion of the board, and the prisoner is pulled completely off their feet.

Below the pelvis, the support board splits to a "Y" to allow the legs to be pulled slightly apart and affixed individually to the rack. Stop when the ankle straps attached to the floor are tight.

The handler should insert one finger between the anchor peg and the prisoner's tail bone. When stretching the legs, the prisoner's crotch is pulled down against the peg; it is critical that the tail bone not be pressed against the peg as this can injure the spine.

The rack is carefully rotated until the tail bone can be felt lightly pressing against the handler's finger, then stopped and locked into place.

A 2 1/2" wide heavy, padded leather strap is then attached to the anchor peg, and laid along the prisoner's spine. The top splits into a forked strap, and each of the two tabs is threaded through anchor points on either side of the prisoner's neck and tightened. The protects the spine from stray blows and assists in restraint.

Leather restraint straps are cinched tightly around the prisoner's lower thighs. With this step, the prisoner should be fully restrained on the rack.

His body will be curved at the hips, with his ass the highest point. The head and back will be very slightly angled downward; this encourages blood flow to the head and helps prevent the prisoner from passing out during severe beatings. The legs are being pulled downward towards the floor at a 45 degree angle, allowing convenient access to the sit spot, crease between the buttocks and thighs, and the upper thighs.

This may sound like a long and complex procedure, but a skilled handler can have a prisoner fully restrained on the rack in about a minute. Since prisoners are often beaten on the rack daily as routine punishment, it is a skill most handlers are very practiced at.

If at any point during the beating you observe shallow, weak breaths or the prisoner complains that he is having difficulty breathing, stop immediately and loosen the straps.

If arms were severely stretched and all straps were cinched as tight as the handler can make them, it would be possible to kill the prisoner due to lack of air. The prisoner can sense this on some level and it adds to the feeling of vulnerability of being on the rack, but the handler must be alert and careful.

Significant pressure is usually put on the restraints to stretch the prisoner's skin and muscles taut for a painful and precise beating. This grows quite painful over time; prisoners have said they felt like they were being stretched on a medieval rack, which is how this device got its name.

Prisoners feel intensely vulnerable in this restraint because of being suspended off the ground on a board narrower than their body, having their joints, muscles, and tendons painfully stretched close to the point of injury, the total immobilization that does not even allow them to move their head, and the actual and potential restriction of breathing.

Handlers may at times use the rack itself as a punishment, for example administering a light beating and then simply leaving the prisoner in the rack for a couple of hours.

BEATING, PART 2: IMPLEMENTS:

Heavy cane: A rubber cane, this is used to cause deep muscle bruising in the buttocks, crease, and thigh (lower six points). This is the only type of bruising that makes it painful for the prisoner to move as he recovers.

It will also leave surface welts, although the rubber design eliminates the severe scarring cuts caused by most other cane materials.

Light cane: Similar to above, but used on the upper four points where lighter musculature is present and the heavy cane might bruise bone or cause nerve damage.

Strap: A double-thickness leather strap, two inches wide and two and a half feet long. Crafted with holes that increase air speed and cause additional tissue damage when skin is forced into them on impact, and hard edges to raise welts.

Considered by most prisoners to be the most painful implement, the strap causes tissue bruising over a large surface area at a shallower level than the muscle bruises caused by the cane.

Used with force, it will turn the prisoner's flesh black and blue, creating bruises that unlike the cane's muscle bruising do not make it painful to move but do make it temporarily painful to sit or lie on the injured area. It also tenderizes and welts the skin.

Flogger: A clump of electrical cords, two and a half feet long, which have been split in half to create individual strands. There is a total of nine strands, a tribute to the cat o' nine tails. The ends of the wires are stripped and the individual copper strands untwisted and spread apart.

This vicious whip stings like a wasp as each of the nine points of impact are struck. The cords leave welts, and the copper ends create hundreds of tiny, almost invisible scrapes and punctures that create an unbearable stinging sensation when laid closely over a large area.

Its primary purpose is surface area skin damage that heals without scarring yet is intensely painful.

Specialty tools: Handlers are issued a wide variety of items to beat prisoners with, including ones designed for use on genitals.

BEATING, PART 3:
INTERVALS:

The standard Hollywood portrayal of beatings, and indeed most household spankings, involves someone being struck rapid-fire with barely any pause between blows. Handlers may do this, but for most purposes should use the program standard 1-minute interval.

When a prisoner is struck, there is a split-second delay, followed by intense pain.

Within 5-10 seconds, that pain becomes slightly less severe, deeper, and felt over a larger area. That deeper pain lasts for 10-20 seconds, then fades dramatically; this is typically the point where the prisoner starts breathing again and the muscles relax slightly.

After another 15-20 seconds, the site becomes tender and starts to throb; at this point the site is far more sensitive to further blows than it would have been earlier.

After one minute, the prisoner has fully felt and processed all stages of pain from the blow, and has time to recover his thoughts enough to begin to dread the next one.

With the 1-minute interval, the prisoner is unable to "blank out" the pain of the beating, and feels each blow fully.

Some handlers find allowing the prisoner to recover in this manner counterintuitive, and feel like the pain would be more severe if the blows were delivered rapid-fire. In fact, while the pain would be more severe, it would be over a far shorter period of time.

If the handler wishes to make the beating more painful, this is supremely easy to do by increasing the number of blows. Advantages of the 1-minute interval:

Prolongs the beating. 60 blows given rapid-fire over ten minutes puts the prisoner in pain and distress for 10 minutes. 60 blows at 1-minute intervals puts the prisoner in pain and distress for an hour.

As the pain from one blow fades, the prisoner has time to anticipate and dread the next.

Sensitizes, rather than numbs, the body.

Causes more overall, prolonged, tolerable suffering that the prisoner fully experiences and comprehends without the prisoner "blocking out" the experience the way he does in a more torturous, intolerable beating. It delivers suffering without causing emotionally traumatic panic.

Encourages the handler to focus on the delivery of each blow.

Facilitates training and rehabilitation, as trainers are encouraged to speak, often gently, to the prisoner about their punishment and future during the recovery intervals. The pain and vulnerability lowers the prisoner's defenses, making them more receptive to the handler's words (as opposed to being "lectured").

BEATING, PART 4: THE STANDARD 10-POINT BEATING:

Prisoner is restrained on the rack, which is designed to restrain the prisoner while stretching skin and muscles tight for more painful and exactly targeted impacts. A skilled handler could place 20 blows on the exact same location if he desired, with the rack preventing unwanted "wiggling" on the part of the prisoner.

Blows are delivered to ten points on the body, five on the left side and five on the right. The points are:

Upper shoulder
Lower shoulder/upper ribcage
Buttocks/sit spot
Crease between buttocks and leg
Top of the upper thigh just below crease.

Blows are administered at one minute intervals. This forces the prisoner to fully experience the pain of each blow, from initial sting to deep ache to throb and burn, as anticipation of the next blow builds.

Handlers usually talk to prisoners about their crimes and why the prisoner deserves the pain inflicted, as well as any attitude problems and misbehaviors that might have earned this beating.

BEATING, PART 5: INTENSIFYING A BEATING:

There are many ways to make a beating more painful:

Wet the prisoner's skin and the implement.

Apply capsicum cream to the skin.

Cross blows; for example with a cane, make an X instead of two parallel stripes.

Strike exactly the same place each time, rather than the general area.

Making the prisoner count the blows is recommended by some handlers.

Previously bruised and welted areas are always more sensitive; a 30-blow beating will be more painful on damaged tissue than the same beating on unmarked skin.

Post-beating intensification: apply salt/vinegar/alcohol solution to prisoner's skin, apply capsicum cream to skin, use front-cuffing and spreader bar to force the prisoner to lie on his back while recovering, or force the prisoner to sit on a hard/painful surface.

BEATING, PART 6: SEVERITY:

It is common for beatings to last 1-2 hours (60-120 blows), and for the prisoner to experience significant pain from being stretched tight on the rack for that length of time. It is impossible to precisely identify the severity of a beating on paper, because of variables such as the prisoner's body type, damage from previous beatings, and force of the blows. These are very general guidelines.

Mild: 30 blows, one with each of the three main implements on each of the 10 points. A very useful routine punishment, often used daily or twice daily (usually morning and evening).

May cause whimpers and moans, but the prisoner is usually mostly silent. This is a painful but easily bearable punishment.

Recovery: prisoners may need a few minutes to catch their breath, and will be sore for a short period, but recovery time is minimal.

Damage: It will leave bruises and welts, but these do not typically cause the prisoner much pain after the beating; often they cannot even feel them.

Moderate: 60 blows, two with each of the three main implements on each of the 10 points. Since pain from beatings tends to increase exponentially with repeated blows, this is approximately four times the severity of a Mild beating. It takes about an hour and is very painful.

Prisoners will whimper, cry, moan, and yelp near the end, though they will rarely scream.

Recovery: Prisoners are usually in shock and pain and are very motionless for about an hour. After that, they will slowly recover to normal behavior, but move gingerly and be reluctant to exercise or place weight on the buttocks. Soreness will last 1-2 days.

Damage: It will cause dramatic bruises, welts, and reddening of the skin from the cuts of the flogger, though the injuries usually look far more painful than they are. Although the marks will take considerable time to fade the prisoner is generally not terribly affected by them after the initial recovery.

Severe: A severe beating would consist of around 120 blows (twelve per point). It takes about two hours and is roughly four times the severity of a Moderate beating.

Expect crying, begging for mercy, and screaming.

Recovery: The prisoner will be very sore and reluctant to move but not completely crippled for at least a week.

Damage: The body will be severely marked with large bruises, overlapping welts, and fine cuts from the flogger, and these injuries will be more severe, painful, and difficult to recover from than those inflicted by a less severe beating.

TORTURE:

Involves around 160 blows (sixteen per point) and lasts nearly three hours. Handlers are reminded not to lessen the force of their blows simply because they are using more of them.

Torture beatings are and should be a form of torture. They make the prisoner scream, sob, beg for it to end, and vocalize uncontrollably. Loss of bladder or bowel control, vomiting, or unconsciousness may occur.

Recovery: Leaves the prisoner semi-crippled and barely mobile for about a week. Diapering must often be used if the prisoner cannot move himself to the toilet.

Damage: Inflicts deep and severe muscle bruising with heavy cane blows that make movement of said muscles severely painful for 1-2 weeks. Bruises tissue badly enough to make it very painful to lie and sit on. Creates a large interlaced network of fine cuts and swollen welts that tighten as they heal, and make moving or flexing the skin extremely painful.

Full recovery will take three weeks to two months, and some permanent scarring is to be expected.

Follow-up: Handlers usually use front-cuffing and a spreader bar (or monitoring and the electric collar) to force the prisoner to lie on his back, and also force sitting for several hours a day following a torture beating.

If used as part of multiple TORTURE punishments for felony violations, it is typical to beat the feet and hands on a separate day to make walking and crawling extremely painful. This temporarily cripples the prisoner and diapers must be used.

Another typical TORTURE punishment in the days following a beating is to force activity to open healing wounds and then massage burning and stinging substances such as capsicum cream into the injuries, a process prisoners find as agonizing as the actual beating when it is done with appropriate lack of mercy.

ELECTRIC SHOCK

Use of electric shock collar: Prisoners usually wear a remotely controlled electric shock collar locked around their neck at all times.

Wearing a collar is quite unpleasant at first, but prisoners eventually learn to ignore it and forget that it is there. In late stages of the program as prisoners become very reliable, prisoners may be weaned off it.

Limits are set individually according to the corrections department's evaluation of prisoner's heart health. TORTURE at high ranges and duration.

There are three collars and two sets of contacts that deliver the electrical charge to the skin which may be used.

The standard contacts were developed for short-haired dogs and are blunt, smooth nubs which protrude 1/2" from the base of the collar. They are irritating at first but not painful. The prisoner is permitted to shift the collar to move the contacts if they become uncomfortable.

The long contacts were designed to penetrate the coat of long-haired and double-coated dogs. They are 3/4" long and taper to a smaller and rounder point. They easily become painful.

The standard collar is nylon, 1 1/2 inches wide, and is placed snugly around the neck. The standard contacts are used. It is adjusted so as not to interfere with breathing or swallowing, but tight enough to keep both contacts in firm contact with the neck at all times.

Prisoners find it very unpleasant at first, but wear it with little or no discomfort once they become accustomed to wearing a snug collar. A light leather collar may be used instead of nylon, and many prisoners prefer the feel of a leather collar, but leather absorbs sweat while nylon is very easy to wash. Most handlers prefer the ease of nylon.

The reward collar is 2" wide, made of soft leather, and lined with ultra-soft plush microfiber fleece. The standard contacts are used. Like the standard collar, it is snug to keep the contacts pressed against the skin.

While a prisoner unused to being collared will not enjoy this one either, experienced prisoners find it blissfully comfortable. Handlers often allow the prisoner to sleep in the reward collar, and sometimes permit prisoners to wear it during the day as well.

The punishment collar is 2 1/2" wide and made of stiff leather. The long contacts are used, and they will press further into the neck. Since the punishment collar does not allow shifting their position, they will become quite painful.

Sores will open under the contacts with prolonged use. The inside of the punishment collar is lined with dozens of staggered 3/8" long, very lightly blunted metal nails. They are all pressed firmly into the neck by the tightness of the collar.

With brief use, the nails should not pierce or scrape the skin, as they have been dulled on the tips. However, with prolonged wear, exertion, and sleeping on the collar, skin sores and scrapes will occur. When this happens, the collar should be removed once a day and antibiotic ointment applied.

The punishment collar is worn tighter than other collars. While it should not restrict breathing, it will be uncomfortably tight around the throat and swallowing and talking will cause pain.

The punishment collar is unpleasant enough to be used for periods as short as an hour. When left on around the clock it is inescapably painful, interferes with the ability to sleep, and quickly wears down resistance of all kinds.

Handlers often apply the punishment collar to new prisoners on arrival for several days to a week to place them in a submissive state.

The shock box should not be placed over the spinal column or larynx; it should be strapped over the thick muscles at the side of the neck. The prisoner is permitted to shift its position when wearing the standard or reward collar to prevent sores from developing under the contacts, but should be reminded that shocks delivered to the spinal column or larynx may cause injury. The shock box should be on one of the sides of the neck at all times.

Shocks are delivered via remote control. When the remote is out of range, the collar can be controlled via a mobile app. The collar also comes with a wide range of preset punishment sequences.

Because of its ability to easily inflict pain that doesn't linger like the pain of a blow, the collar is an invaluable training tool for quick, minor punishments during training. It is also used as the primary tool to force prisoners to comply with restraints, orders, and exercise.

Sleep deprivation:

Sometimes accomplished through the use of stress positions, this is most effortlessly inflicted through the sleep deprivation program on the prisoner's shock collar. It will automatically deliver timed shocks sufficient to prevent the prisoner from sleeping for more than a few minutes.

The program automatically increases the frequency and intensity of shocks as time wears on.

Limited to 80 hours, TORTURE at 72 hours. 48 hours recommended as a standard punishment. Often combined with pain; if the handler does not want to be involved, the shock collar routines Sleep Deprivation/Mild, Sleep Deprivation/Moderate, or Sleep Deprivation/SEVERE may be activated.

Sleep deprivation should be carried out in isolation (Cell or Torture Chamber) and is generally combined with diet restriction.

An important note on shock collar use (and abuse):

The shock collar and beatings are the most frequently used (and advised) methods of control, discipline, and punishment. Handlers leave an electric shock collar on their prisoners at all times.

Because of the collar's ability to render the prisoner screaming in the fetal position at the tap of a button, it is an invaluable control tool for obtaining instant and complete submission.

At lower levels, a punishment severe enough that the prisoner will work very hard to avoid it is also a mere press of a button. Programmed punishment routines deliver more prolonged, carefully developed punishment up to torture levels without any involvement on the part of the handler.

However, it is the collar's very ease of use that makes it prone to misuse. The majority of instances where the department has been forced to remove a prisoner from his handler have involved abuse of the shock collar. The shock collar can easily induce overwhelming fear in the prisoner.

The prisoner should be very afraid of disobeying his handler and of violating rules. He should never be afraid OF his handler. He should be afraid of the punishments his handler can inflict, but develop intense trust of his handler over time. Fairness and empathy are as important in a handler as sadism.

If a prisoner fears his handler's presence or temper, those are signs of abuse and the prisoner will be pulled from the handler and the handler terminated.

Why are shock collars so prone to abuse?

When you beat the prisoner, you feel the force you use in your swing, see its impact on the prisoner's body, and see the damage you inflict in terms of redness, bruising, and cuts. It's easy to read those signs and moderate your force so that it is not unbearable for your prisoner.

Handlers rarely beat their prisoners to the point of uncontrollable screaming, yet will easily inflict that level of pain with the collar.

SHOCK COLLARS CAUSE EXTREME PAIN AND STRESS. While it may not leave marks, this pain is real, deeply felt, and fully experienced mentally by the prisoner.

They affect the entire body, temporarily taking over the nervous system. This is severely disconcerting, the muscle contractions are exhausting, and there is nothing the prisoner can do mentally to distract from the pain of the shock because it is so fast and invades the nervous system.

If a shock collar is overused, or used simply because the handler feels like it, the prisoner will come to fear the handler and will experience lasting generalized trauma not related to their own behavior. This will get your prisoner pulled, and you will be terminated for abuse. If you notice the prisoner flinching, trembling, or cowering in your presence, evaluate your use of the shock collar.

If you want to hurt your prisoner, you are allowed and encouraged to beat them. This is considered part of their sentence. Because of the greater contact and empathy, as well as being a more endurable if often severe form of pain, it is less likely to cause trauma.

RESTRAINT AND STRESS POSITIONS

Restraint:

May be used to bind prisoner's limbs together or to secure the prisoner to a fixed object, or both. Integral in stress positions, used to restrain the prisoner for painful punishments, or simply used as routine punishment. Prisoners should be restrained frequently and for prolonged periods of time.

The wrists and ankles are the only place where permanent scarring is permitted on a routine basis; virtually all prisoners emerge with scars from restraint, which often fade over the years.

Prisoners typically experience abrasions, sores, welts, and cuts to the wrists and ankles on a continual basis due to the heavy use of restraints. This is normal and expected.

Handlers should apply antibiotic ointment and antiseptics regularly to open wounds, but they are not bandaged. These injuries are typically very painful when the prisoner is wearing restraints, but prisoners easily learn to ignore them while unrestrained.

Temporary nerve damage to the wrists usually results from the heavy use of handcuffs. This may numb portions of the prisoner's hands or make them tingle uncomfortably. Such symptoms usually resolve within a year of exiting the program.

Use of police handcuffs, leg irons, and belly chains is encouraged on a regular basis as they make the prisoner feel like a prisoner. It's easy to underestimate how much pain being restrained by these simple devices causes.

Long periods spent in snug handcuffs can be difficult to endure, and they have many variants like hinged, weighted, and rigid cuffs that are more severe than normal cuffs.

Handlers are well equipped with a large variety of restraints and may order additional ones. It would be impossible to list them all here.

Spreader bars: Typically used on the ankles to hold the legs open (very useful for genital punishments), they may be applied to thighs and wrists as well. Many are adjustable in how far apart the limbs are spread.

Weighted shackles: One weighted shackle is installed in the Cell. The handler has additional weighted wrist, ankle, and neck shackles available. Weighted shackles elicit a powerful feeling of restraint in the prisoner.

Yoke: Similar to a spreader bar, the yoke is a straight, heavy metal bar with openings for the prisoner's neck and wrists. The wrists are held away from the body and up at the level of the neck. The prisoner is usually forced to sit, stand, or walk in the yoke.

Sit - Stay: A straight iron rod with integrated rigid shackles for the ankles, wrists, and neck. Keeps the prisoner immobile in a cramped sitting position.

Collars: Metal, chain, and spiked collars, including ones that make it impossible for the prisoner to lie down or lower their head.

Rope: Useful for more unusual and detailed restraint than steel restraints allow for.

Leather restraints: Generally broad, soft, and pleasant to wear, leather restraints can be used to reward good behavior while still reminding the prisoner he is under your control.

Bungee cords: Used to put pressure on restraints.

Hand pinions: A metal frame in the shape of a flat hand that straps to the wrist. Each finger is placed in a u-shaped curve in the frame and a screw is tightened down on the finger to hold the hand open.

The screw pressure may be made somewhat painful, but be cautious as it would be easy to injure the prisoner. The main point of this device is to hold the hands open so that the prisoner can be strapped on the palms.

Mitts: Available in painful and non-painful versions, these completely encase the hands in fingerless mitts rendering them useless. They prevent the prisoner from undoing straps, removing anal plugs, etc. Useful for cart work when you don't want to handcuff the prisoner, but also don't want to risk him unhitching himself when your back is turned.

Temporary crippling with leg irons: The prisoner is ordered to extend his toes like a ballet dancer. This relaxes the Achilles tendon and makes the ankle much smaller than it is when standing. Leg irons are then tightened low around the ankles; they should be very snug but not tight enough to restrict circulation. The prisoner cannot stand or walk.

It isn't merely painful to stand or walk, it is physically impossible because the tendon cannot be contracted. This restraint is not terribly painful, no more so than any extended use of leg irons. It is demoralizing and causes increased submission because prisoners can only crawl; getting on and off the bed and using the toilet are difficult.

Gagging: A wide variety of gags may be used with the functions of holding the jaws open to create soreness, drying the mouth, preventing vocalization, inflicting pain on the tongue and roof of the mouth, inflicting pain on the corners of the mouth, forcing the prisoner to dissolve a foul-tasting tablet in the mouth, to force the prisoner to ingest liquid, or to activate a prisoner's gag reflex.

Stress positions:

"Stress positions" is a term used to a broad category of torture techniques. Within the context of the program, a stress position is simply the act of restraining a prisoner in a manner that becomes uncomfortable or painful more rapidly than simply handcuffing them or placing them in leg irons.

Handlers may use "real" stress positions, where the prisoner is forced to stand in an agonizingly difficult pose under threat of punishment until they collapse and are punished before being ordered back into the position. However, this practice is discouraged because it fosters distrust of the handler.

Giving impossible orders (like maintaining a stress position) that are certain to be disobeyed and punished is extremely damaging to the prisoner's attitude and desire to please his handler.

Obedience must always be an option; this is also why anal plugs are always used to hold in enemas. Ordering the prisoner to do something that hurts him is a valuable training tool; making him fail orders is the opposite.

Handlers are extensively trained on avoiding injury while inflicting stress positions. These positions are numerous and not all listed here. Refer to training for specific limits of tightness, positioning, and length of time in various restraints.

Common program stress positions:

Prisoner's arms are cuffed behind his back, and a chain attached to the cuffs is pulled up (towards the ceiling), straining the prisoner's shoulders and arms.

Prisoner is hogtied, with his wrists and ankles pulled together behind his back, forcing the prisoner into a reverse bowed position.

Prisoner is spread-eagled on the floor or standing.

Prisoners hands are cuffed in front, and a chain attached to the cuffs is pulled up (towards the ceiling), stretching the arms high above the head. To make this position even more painful, the handler may raise the cuffs high enough that the prisoner is forced to stand tiptoe on the balls of his feet.

PRESSURE, COMPRESSION, AND CLAMPING

Use of pinch collar for dogs and other pronged or spiked devices: Must not tear or pierce skin, with the exception of the provided punishment shock collar, shackles, and belts.

Pinching and compression: Use of approved clamps on skin, including nipples, lips, ears, and genitals. May be used to restrain and as a stress position aid. Do not use anything but provided light clamps for more than 30 minutes without a 10 minute period for circulation to restore.

Light clamps are initially minimally painful, but will cause significant pain after several hours and may be left on for up to 24 hours.

Forcing to sit on painful or uncomfortable surfaces: Virtually always done after beating the buttocks, and usually naked. The Tomb is an example of this. Additional techniques include having the prisoner sit naked on the spiked side of a floor mat, rocks, a narrow board, industrial metal catwalk flooring, or jacks.

Spiked belts: Locking leather straps lined with short nail-like spikes, of very similar design to the punishment shock collar. Typically applied to the top of the chest directly under the arms, the chest across pecs and nipples, the upper ribcage, the lower ribcage, stomach, waist, and upper and lower thighs.

May cause minor scrapes and punctures but have been carefully designed by the corrections department to avoid lasting injury while inflicting intense discomfort. Properly applied, they make it very painful to breathe but do not restrict air intake.

TEMPERATURE AND SENSATION

Application of ginger or capsicum based substances to the skin (excluding eyes and nose) and genitals:

Capsicum ointment makes the prisoner feel as though his skin is being severely burned, but causes no injury. May be used to sensitize the skin prior to or after a beating.

Also used to intensify the pain of sitting, restraints, clamps, and hot showers.

Virtually any punishment involving blows, abrasion, or pressure is made magnitudes more painful by simple application of capsicum ointment.

TORTURE when inserted into anus or urethra with an object used to "fuck" the prisoner repeatedly, which is far more agonizing than simply applying some cream to the rectum.

May also be TORTURE when used over large portions of the body or on open wounds depending on their number and severity.

Merely rubbing capsicum cream into a prisoner's restraint-welted ankles is not considered torture. Applying it over the entire back and buttocks including the genitals after a severe beating has left hundreds of open wounds on those areas would be considered torture.

Ginger is usually used in whole, fresh root form, although a fresh juice is also available. Usually, a large section of ginger root is peeled and inserted into the prisoner's anus for an unbearable stinging, burning sensation which is intensified by any friction or clenching.

Some handlers enjoy gingering the prisoner before a beating, which tends to force them to clench on the root. Many creative variations of ginger punishment are possible.

Application of vinegar, salt, and alcohol solution to broken skin: May be used to disinfect open restraint and beating wounds up to three times daily when additional pain is desired. Use antibiotic ointment (plain soothing or chili pepper treated) or antiseptic on open wounds at least twice a day.

Very hot or cold showers: Limited to safe settings on shower unit, which pelts the prisoner painfully hard with either very hot or very cold water. The force of the water on a punishment setting feels miserable on the wounds inflicted by beatings, and other tenderized skin.

If used to induce hypothermia, prisoner must be warmed after one hour. Cold showers may not be used prior to placement in The Tomb, as that would lower body temperature dangerously. Brief cold showers may be used before placing prisoner naked in The Cell or Torture Chamber.

Hot showers may not be used immediately prior to or after exercise due to heat stroke risk.

GENITALS AND DIGESTIVE TRACT

Sexual denial: Prisoners are not allowed to masturbate at any time while in the program. Some handlers use chastity cages, while others choose to leave temptation open to punishment.

Prisoners are thus in a frequent state of unfulfilled sexual arousal and handlers may edge them, stimulating them to near-orgasm and then denying release. They may also punish erections or orgasms.

Sounding (insertion of sterile objects into urethra): Sounding, properly applied, is not terribly painful. It does, however, cause enormous distress and fear. It renders prisoners intensely vulnerable, and creates sensations that are very intense.

Prisoners will often make mewing noises, buck against restraints, and gasp, not from pain but simply intense and overwhelming sensation. Some prisoners consider sounding to be one of the worst sensations possible, while others find it arousing.

Often, a sounding rod will be left in the urethra for up to eight hours to block urination. Prisoners will usually experience a burning sensation when urinating for a couple days after sounding.

Insertion of objects into the anus: Anal plugs are the most common form of anal punishment. They are often used to cause a painful stretching sensation to the anal sphincter.

Anal plugs may be left in for up to twelve hours, and reinserted after one hour and ample opportunity for elimination.

A dildo may be repeatedly thrust in and out of the anus.

A vibrator or other stimulation can be applied to the prisoner's prostate, usually as a form of sexual denial.

Ginger roots may be inserted for intense burning sensation.

Any safe item may be inserted into the anus, provided it does not cause tearing of the skin.

Application of rings and weights to testicles: Testicle rings are generally made with one of two purposes in mind; stretching the scrotum tissue between the groin and the balls, or placing weight on the testicles. They can range from mild to unbearable.

Stretchers may be metal tubes (sometimes internally spiked), or a series of many round bands, added until the scrotum is painfully stretched with no more room to add additional rings.

A minor stretch may be applied for daily or long-term wear, causing discomfort and occasional mild pain. On the other end of the spectrum, a severe stretch can render the prisoner immobile in agony.

Weights are usually used with the prisoner standing or walking; usually in a standing position with their arms restrained high above their heads and their ankles in a spreader bar to keep the legs open.

Weight is applied to the testicles by a ring around the scrotum above the balls, tying a rope around the scrotum above the balls, or by means of a conical, internally spiked device that resembles a miniature "cone of shame" collar for post-surgical pets, which is also affixed above the testicles. The handler then attaches weights which dangle from the scrotum. Like stretchers, this may range from mild to unbearable agony.

The handler may also strike the weights, making them swing painfully. He can attach weights with long enough ropes that they lie on the floor, and force the prisoner to walk, dragging the weights with his testicles.

Handlers can also padlock the testicles, simply placing the hasp of a padlock around the scrotum above the testicles and locking it. This is very uncomfortable but not terribly painful, and can be a very potent psychological reminder to the prisoner of his status. The prisoner can thus be chained to the wall by his balls as well.

Use of a humbler on testicles to force kneeling: A humbler resembles a set of stocks for the testicles. Two halves of a smooth wooden board are locked together to trap the testicles. The prisoner is ordered to get on hands and knees, the testicles are pulled back between his legs, and secured in the humbler which rests flat against the upper thighs.

The prisoner cannot stand or otherwise extend his body without inflicting agonizing pulling pain on the scrotum. Because it forces the prisoner to kneel, it is called the humbler.

Resting the weight on the hands and knees on a hard floor can quickly become painful, and can damage the joints. If the prisoner is to be left in the humbler for any appreciable period of time or made to crawl, it should be on a padded surface.

The humbler is less practical for longer restraint than it is for restraining the prisoner in a kneeling position for punishments like figging, enemas, and beating the buttocks. In situations like that, it is usually used in combination with a spreader bar to hold the legs open wide.

Enemas: The prisoner is generally restrained, and two quarts of water slowly inserted into the bowels via the anus. The prisoner will have an uncontrollable urge to defecate within minutes, and generally be unable to control his bowels.

The prisoner may be allowed to defecate, or an inflatable anal plug may be inserted to force retention of the enema for a maximum of one hour. This is extraordinarily unpleasant, and prisoners often beg for release, moaning and whining in discomfort.

For a more severe punishment, use the safe irritants provided by the Corrections Department, which come in two varieties. One increases cramping to very painful levels, and the other makes the enema "burn" on the way out.

The cramping irritant will cause the prisoner to beg passionately for release and vocalize his misery to an almost amusing extent. Only sounding comes close to a retained cramping enema when it comes to reducing a prisoner to a pleading supplicant. Use of cold water can also make retaining the enema more unpleasant.

The burning enema loses much of its impact when an anal ring is used; since it hurts so badly on the way out, there is no need to force retention. Simply sit the prisoner on the toilet, and let them choose when to release their bowels and endure the pain. Generally, they will release quickly the first time they experience one, but much more reluctantly thereafter.

Limited to 3 enemas in a 24-hour period and 14 per week; however, those three enemas may be administered consecutively. May not be used daily for more than two weeks.

Cramping enemas must be used with an anal ring to hold the rectum open upon release preventing hemorrhoids from excess straining.

Application of laxatives, including those modified by the corrections department to cause severe cramping: Cramping laxative must be used with an anal ring to hold the rectum open preventing hemorrhoids from excess straining. An anal plug should be used as well until release is allowed.

Limited to once every two weeks if severe cramping is induced, once per week if not. Enemas provide a similar sensation while being safe to use more freely.

Control and delay of urination: Prisoners are required to ask permission from their handler before using the toilet.

Handers may require the prisoner to "hold it" for up to 8 hours. Prisoner may be forced to ingest water to intensify bladder discomfort. A urethral sound may be inserted to plug the bladder, or the prisoner may be catheterized and the catheter used to control urine flow.

Inserting a too-large catheter and leaving it in for 24 hours, draining the bladder every 6 hours while forcing the prisoner to over-hydrate is a prolonged and very uncomfortable punishment especially suited to offenses such as failing to ask to use the toilet or failing to retain urine in the bladder when ordered.

Control and delay of defecation:
Prisoners are required to ask permission from their handler before using the toilet.

Handlers may require the prisoner to "hold it" for up to 24 hours. They may intensify the discomfort through the use of an inflatable butt plug to make the bowel feel fuller.

The handler may also administer laxatives and require the prisoner to wait for up to 3 hours before elimination. As this is often physically impossible for the prisoner to do on his own, a butt plug should be used to prevent uncontrolled bowel release.

Diapering: While this should not be done merely to humiliate the prisoner, diapers may be used when in situations where they will be unable to use the toilet for a long period of time.

Punishment horse: This was a common military POW punishment in olden days, and often rendered prisoners unable to walk. The modern, blunted and widened version provided by the Corrections Department does not cause the severe tissue and nerve damage common to the original model.

The 4' long "back" of the horse is formed by boards set in a triangular shape, with the "spine" of the horse being the peak of the triangle. Prisoners are forced to straddle it naked, and the cock and balls are placed forward and butt cheeks are spread.

The triangular shape forces the legs apart as though the prisoner is riding a horse. A good portion of the prisoner's weight is placed on his perineum, causing severe pain.

The legs do not touch the ground, and are tied down to the floor. The prisoner is typically back-cuffed while "riding," and will be still and largely silent; the horse can cause very severe pain, but the prisoner is usually focused on not moving so as not to make it worse.

Do not underestimate the pain being inflicted. Handlers should gauge pain level and when to end the punishment not by vocalizations or squirming, but how frozen in place he is. Prisoners left on the horse for an entire hour usually appear to be trying not to so much as breathe.

Pressure on the nerves causes blood flow to the genitals to be restricted, which causes additional pain.

An agonizing point in the punishment is when the prisoner is removed from the horse and blood rushes back to the genitals causing severely painful pins and needles. Prisoners may be reluctant to dismount because of the pain of doing so.

Limited to one hour to prevent nerve damage.

Genital stapling: A sterile surgical stapler meant for closing wounds as an alternative to stitches makes an excellent tool to staple lips and other tissue together. While this procedure hurts, it is not as painful as prisoners generally fear.

While some handlers may apply staples simply for the psychological distress the procedure causes, it is usually used to staple the foreskin so that it cannot retract or stretch, causing severe pain to the stapled areas when the prisoner has an erection.

Must be removed every week, for cleaning of the penis, but may be immediately reapplied after cleaning. Often used long-term as a means of sexual control. Antiseptic should be applied daily.

Elastration: Placement of a rubber livestock castration band around the upper scrotum. This cuts blood supply to the testicles and grows increasingly painful with time.

It is also quite painful to remove, as the prisoner will experience intense "pins and needles" as blood supply and nerve operation is restored. Strictly limited to 45 minutes as this procedure will castrate the prisoner if left for long enough to kill tissue.

May be repeated after one hour.

Application of nasal-gastric tube larger than medically necessary: Must be inflicted by a medical professional. Causes very unpleasant choking, gagging, and pain. May not be left in longer than four hours. May be used by a medical professional to simply feed the prisoner if they are refusing food or water.

TORTURE if used to administer stomach-filling liquid with laxative and cramping agent to painfully empty prisoner's entire digestive system, usually followed by punitive diet restriction.

This punishment is applied while fully restrained over the toilet, takes 3-4 hours, and has been compared to the pain of contractions in childbirth. It causes dehydration as well as muscle failure due to exhaustion, and the prisoner will be debilitated by weakness and muscle soreness for several days afterward.

This is usually used to the handler's advantage to extend the punishment by giving water only via IV and placing the prisoner on a starvation diet. Since the prisoner's digestive tract is completely empty, hunger pangs are severe and start almost immediately.

This is generally a devastating punishment because it is not simply painful; it punishes the prisoner's entire body on multiple fronts for a significant period of time. Prisoners will often do anything to avoid a repeat.

DIETARY RESTRICTION AND TASTE AVERSION

Calorie and diet restriction: See nutrition manual for details and restrictions. In general, food intake may, for behavioral punishment purposes, be restricted to liquid protein drinks produced for the purpose by the corrections department. They contain the necessary vitamins, fat, calories, and electrolytes to sustain health while being unpleasantly flavored and minimally satisfying, leaving the prisoner constantly hungry.

Flavors include hot chili, unflavored, and bitter. Prisoners may also be starved or given lower than normal calories in a manner dictated by the nutrition manual. Prisoners should be fed a normal diet when not being punished.

Placement of unpleasantly flavored items in mouth: Limited to those provided by the corrections department, which have been tested for safety.

Available flavors: Hot chili (causes significant pain for 45 minutes to 2 hours), bitter, ginger, soap, and saccharine. In gag form in which a chunk of the substance is held in the mouth until dissolved, or in a convenient spray.

EXERCISE

Overexertion: Prisoner is forced to exercise beyond their comfortable strength and/or cardiovascular limits. Cart pulling, a treadmill, or repeated push-ups are examples.

The most popular form of this punishment is pulling a cart, which may be weighted and/or the prisoner may be required to pull it for long distances or run while pulling the cart.

Self-infliction of pain: Prisoner is forced to perform actions which aggravate injuries, restraints, or pressure devices. Walking on bruised feet, pulling a rope with beaten palms, walking in pronged shackles, and dragging a weight attached to the testicles are all examples of this.

CART TRAINING AND PULLING

The standard four-wheeled cart is relatively lightweight. The prisoner is harnessed and bridled with a bit in his mouth, and the harness affixed to the traces. The handler sits on the cart and commands the prisoner through reins and vocal cues. The cart is invaluable for exercising, training, and punishing prisoners as well as teaching attentiveness to and trust of the handler.

Pulling the cart, stopping it, and maneuvering it as well as interpreting and obeying cues given by the bit are foreign tasks and surprisingly challenging and stressful to learn.

With the handler seated behind the prisoner, the prisoner must learn to be steered from behind with no body language cues. Handlers should spend a number of weeks patiently training the prisoner on how to respond to all cues and combinations of cues before attempting to use pulling the cart as a punishment.

Even when done gently, the training alone is an exhausting and physically distressing ordeal. The discomfort caused by the bit, and the attention to it that the task requires, are very punishing in themselves.

When training is complete, handlers are encouraged to use the cart as a reward as well as a punishment. Getting to be outdoors in the fresh air and get exercise can be very pleasant and a much-needed way to keep the prisoner somewhat integrated with the outside world.

A gentle walk through the park can do wonders to help prisoners cope with the stress of the program and learn to trust their handlers.

The cart is an excellent tool for punishing and exhausting the prisoner. He may be made to pull the cart for a long period of time with his hands cuffed behind him to cause additional pain, and denied food, water, and bathroom breaks while he is hitched. Handlers may also make the prisoner wear an anal plug while hitched.

Prisoners can be forced to jog or sprint to exhaustion while pulling the cart, often alternated with walking. A small trailer is easily hitched to the back of the cart and weighted to make the cart difficult to pull; this becomes especially difficult when the prisoner is made to walk up and down hills.

Hauling construction gravel for the city is one particularly useful and exhausting punishment. Because he must remain attentive to the bit at all times, this is mentally as well as physically taxing. Since it is done outdoors with the prisoner's upper body bare except for the harness, elements like sun, heat, cold, and hail can also add to the prisoner's discomfort.

SUGGESTED STANDARD PUNISHMENTS

These are some easy, go-to punishments. All handlers will develop favorites of their own. A volume of handler-submitted punishment ideas and suggestions may be compiled in the future.

Concrete and steel treatment: Place prisoner naked in The Cell wearing leg irons, belly chain, and front handcuffs. No comfort or entertainment items provided. 24 hours, with 8 working hours spent back-cuffed, is usually very effective. The cage within the cell may also be used.

The human body is soft, and susceptible to pressure, and demands a free range of movement. It is very foreign to a human being to be in an environment where nothing gives, and to have unyielding pressure applied to the body especially with limbs restrained.

The concrete and steel treatment causes discomfort, pain, and general distress, and generally becomes difficult to bear after 4 hours.

Three-Stage, 10-point beating: Prisoner is placed in the restraint rack and beaten on each of the standard ten points, first with the cane, then with the strap, then with the flogger. The handler will select the number of blows with each implement.

Spiked restraints: Spiked leather straps one and a half inches wide are tightened around the prisoner's chest under the arms, over the nipples, and around the upper and lower ribcage. Properly tightened, these do not interfere with breathing, but make it intensely painful.

Additional spiked straps are tightened around the stomach, waist and upper and lower thighs. Neck, wrists, and ankles are placed in heavy, custom-fitted spiked metal collar and shackles.

Prisoner may be left to suffer, or forced to walk, or placed in stress positions.

Dry mouth gagging: A popular punishment is to insert a rubber bit gag to hold the prisoner's mouth open, then clamp the nose shut. This forces the prisoner to breathe through his open mouth, quickly drying the mouth and throat painfully.

When combined with hot pepper sprays to the mouth and throat, this is a brutally effective punishment especially if the prisoner is denied water for some time afterward.

Diet restriction: Limit prisoner's food intake to two punishment drinks per day for 2-5 days.

Wearing of punishment collar for 24-36 hours: This collar is annoying and painful, often enough to interfere with sleep. It becomes more painful the longer it is worn. Frequent application of electric shock recommended.

Sleep deprivation, 48 hours: No food provided, supply bottled water of a quantity sufficient for 48 hours. Set collar to Sleep Deprivation/Moderate for regular administration of pain. Place prisoner in Torture Chamber with lights on high and leave prisoner in isolation for duration of punishment.

Electric punishment sequences:
Designed to inflict intense pain over a period of 1 hour, this is similar to a beating but without any effort required.

Mild sequence will leave the prisoner exhausted from the frequent shocks and their muscle spasms.

Moderate is difficult to endure.

Severe will make the prisoner writhe and scream frequently for the duration, and they will be unable to stand for a couple of hours afterward.

TORTURE sequence is administered while fully restrained and lasts for 8 hours with frequent shocks ranging from mild to severe preventing the prisoner from resting. Screams are frequent and blood-curdling.

Prisoner will be unable to walk for some time afterword, will have generalized and intense muscle pain for several days, and be dehydrated and exhausted. Some longer lasting muscle strains may be inflicted. Expect to see minor burns at prong sites.

Spread-eagle stretch: A spiked plastic chair mat is laid on the floor of the Chamber, spikes facing up. The prisoner is ordered to lie on his back on the mat in the spread-eagle position.

Handcuffs and leg irons are used to secure the prisoner in the spread-eagle pose, without straining the prisoner's muscles. Then bungee cords are affixed to the cuffs and leg irons, and stretched taut to anchor points.

The prisoner must allow his arms and legs to be stretched painfully if he wishes to relieve the pressure on the restraints, but he is able to pull them into more bearable positions to prevent injury to the muscles and ligaments - it just hurts his ankles and wrists.

1-4 hours is typically recommended; this punishment is hard on the body.

Cart pulling: Hitch the prisoner to the cart wearing an anal plug and cruncher bit. Cuff his hands behind his back. Force him to jog until exhausted, shocking him when he falters. Make him walk the cart while he catches his breath, then force him to jog again. Repeat this sequence until the prisoner is near the point of muscle failure.

Submission therapy: If a prisoner is becoming defiant or otherwise needs to be made more submissive towards the handler, this works virtually every time. Some handlers "welcome" their new prisoners home with this treatment.

This was an early handler discovery when he was working with a very defiant prisoner, and its widespread effectiveness for a very specific purpose prompted the suggestion of the development of a handler-submitted punishment list which may be released in the future.

Start by administering three cramping enemas in a row. Force each enema to be held for up to an hour; the prisoner will beg, plead, and supplicate himself to you in desperation for release. When the enemas are finished insert a large butt plug.

Catheterize the prisoner, using an overly large catheter. Its difficult, painful insertion will

24 hours of lying sprawled on the cement floor, unable to stand, speak, or use his hands, his balls chained to the wall, a large plug in his repeatedly enema-punished ass, a painful catheter in his penis removing control of his bladder, a tight collar around his neck, having to beg with the most pleading of noises to have his full bladder emptied will make the prisoner overwhelmingly vulnerable and submissive.

The results are so good that some handlers do this once a month as a maintenance measure because they enjoy how pliable the prisoner becomes afterward.

CHAPTER FOUR

No Turning Back

Neal walked to the toilet at the corner of the cell and retched. He was shaking in dread at the idea of such treatment, and inconceivably, aroused. Unlike many of his fellow lifers, he didn't consider himself a tough guy. He had no illusions about being able to endure the horrific punishments outlined in the manual without crying, screaming, and begging.

He would have to place himself utterly at the mercy of his handler and pray to every entity ever imagined that he got someone who would show at least some restraint in torturing him, and give him a chance to earn punishments he could bear instead of ones that left him catatonic on the floor in a pool of his own urine.

After reading that, he could well imagine the state of exhausted pain that the agent had described. He wouldn't be himself, just a puppet to endure his handler's whims. The agent had mentioned more experienced handlers preferring submissive, cooperative prisoners, and had seemed to indicate an experienced handler might have a more even hand with punishing him.

Neal drew in a shaky breath, utterly terrified. He could get an inexperienced, complete sadist. He was going to have to enter training with the goal of pleasing his trainers at all costs. He could worry about dignity, pride, and the triumph of the human spirit later. Right now, he absolutely had to attract the best handler possible despite his inevitable pain and fear at the training center with the overriding message, *I'll be good. Please adopt me. I'll do anything under the sun to please you.*

Neal signed the papers with an unsteady hand, then walked back to the toilet and threw up. The next years of his life were going to be.... interesting.

CHAPTER FIVE

More Reading

I hope you enjoyed the book!

Reviews are essential to the success of the series on amazon, so if you would like to see it continue, even the briefest of positive comments will make a huge difference. An actual "book review" is not needed; a simple, "I liked it!" comment works great too!

To check out the rest of the series so far, visit amazon.com and search to view all books by Eli Harder.

If you are an avid reviewer and would like to receive free review copies of future books in the series, shoot an email to AuthorEliHarder@gmail.com. You can also contact him at that address with requests for scenes in future books and to get on his mailing list to be notified of future releases.

Made in the USA
Monee, IL
14 May 2024

58383550R00069